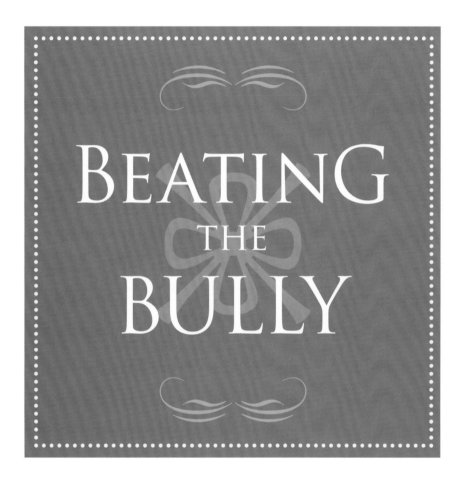

BEATING
THE
BULLY

STORY BY MICHAEL J. MCLELLAND

PAINTINGS BY ANDREA COPE KIRK

ISBN 13: 978-1-59955-006-0

Published by CFI, an imprint of Cedar Fort, Inc.
2373 W. 700 S., Springville, UT, 84663
Distributed by Cedar Fort, Inc., www.cedarfort.com

LIBRARY OF CONGRESS CATALOGING-IN-PUBLICATION DATA

McLelland, Michael J., 1949-
  Beating the bully / by Michael J. McLelland ; illustrated by Andrea C. Kirk.
    p. cm.
  Summary: Tired of being bullied, a boy vows to get revenge, but when the opportunity presents itself, he decides to be kind instead.
  ISBN 978-1-59955-006-0
  [1. Bullies. 2. Stories in rhyme.] I. Kirk, Andrea Cope, ill. II. Title.

  PZ8.3.M228Be 2007
  [E]--dc22

                    2006039285

Jacket and book design by Nicole Williams
Cover design © 2007 by Lyle Mortimer
Edited by Kimiko M. Hammari

Printed on acid-free paper

Printed in China
10   9   8   7   6   5   4   3   2   1

AUTHOR
DEDICATION

To all those who I bullied and to those who bullied me.
You were the inspiration for this book.

ILLUSTRATOR
DEDICATION

To my three brothers, Tyler, Jared, and Kevin. Tyler and
Jared, your constant teasing as children has given me
adequate inspiration for my paintings. Thank you for
making me tough. Kevin, I'm sorry for teasing you.

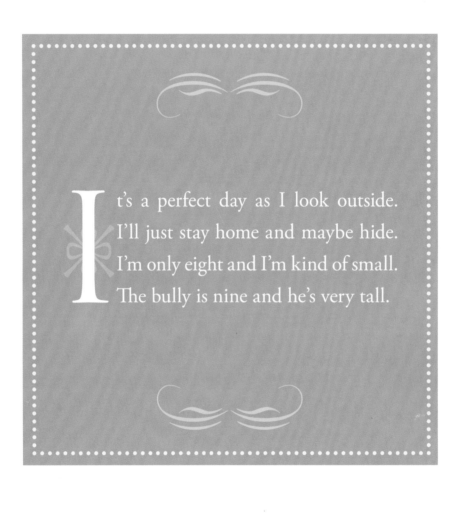

It's a perfect day as I look outside.
I'll just stay home and maybe hide.
I'm only eight and I'm kind of small.
The bully is nine and he's very tall.

MRS. KIRK
ART

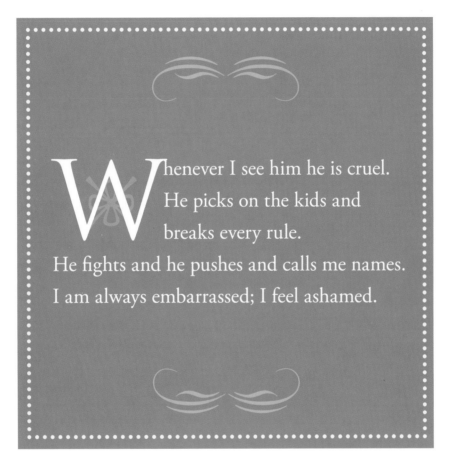

Whenever I see him he is cruel.
He picks on the kids and
breaks every rule.
He fights and he pushes and calls me names.
I am always embarrassed; I feel ashamed.

I really hate going to church or to school.
He's always waiting to bully or fool.
I can't tell my mom or even my dad.
I know if I do he will be worse than bad.

My life is just awful; I need change.
Now is the time for me to arrange
To work out and eat food
that is healthy and right.
It will take a long time but my goal is in sight.

Time passes so fast; it really can fly.
I look in the mirror and I take a deep sigh.
I like what I see as I gaze in the mirror:
Strong muscles; I'm tall; my eyes show no fear.

Today is the day that I even the score.
I'll punch out his lights, put him flat
on the floor.
I'll call him mean names and make
him feel bad.
This will be the best day that I've ever had.

I find him alone walking home from our school. I stride up to him cause I now feel real cool. I tell him it's time now to pay his price. I'll hit him once and then maybe twice.

He is going to find out what
it's like to feel pain.
I am going to hurt him;
I will not restrain.
I look in his eyes and I now see his fear.
He starts to sob; I see my face
in the mirror.

I have now become bully and he
is now me.
I remember my pain, begging even
each plea.
This isn't how I thought the
punishment would feel.
The more I scared him, my hurt
became real.

What am I thinking? Whose
pain would I add?
There are plenty of people
who feel really bad.
More bullies are not what the
universe needs.
There should be more kind people
who do kind deeds.

Just when my foe thinks I'll hit him and hurt,
I hug his shoulder and straighten his shirt.
I tell him I'm sorry; he can't pay the price.
I'm not a bully; I'd rather be nice.

Go home and learn to leave
others alone.
There's no gain in hurting
or making folks moan.
I've just learned a familiar rule is true:
Do unto others, what you'd want
done to you.

That was the day that the bullies got beat.
I enjoyed watching their hasty retreat.
There are two fewer bullies in our world today.
The price of revenge was just too high to pay.

I look back at childhood, a long time ago.
The closest of friends seem to come and to go.
It's funny the bully is still my best friend.
I'm thankful I took the right path in the end.